Grrrrrrrr!

Freddie turned slowly. He found himself staring at the face of a German shepherd. "Nice boy," he whispered.

Grrrrrrrrrrrrrrrrrrrr.

A couple of boxes stood between the dog and Freddie. About twenty feet behind Freddie was the fire door he'd come through. If he pushed over the boxes, he'd distract the dog.

Freddie took a deep breath. Then he shoved the boxes with all his might. He raced for the door. There would be no time to pull it shut.

The dog was right behind him—and getting

Books in The New Bobbsey Twins series

Available from MINSTREL Books

THE NEW
Bobbsey
Twins™
#2
THE CASE OF THE RUNAWAY MONEY

LAURA LEE HOPE
ILLUSTRATED BY GEORGE TSUI

A MINSTREL® BOOK

PUBLISHED BY POCKET BOOKS

New York   London   Toronto   Sydney   Tokyo

A MINSTREL PAPERBACK *ORIGINAL*

 A Minstrel Book published by
Pocket Books, a division of Simon & Schuster Inc.
1230 Avenue of the Americas, New York, NY 10020

Copyright © 1987 by Simon & Schuster Inc.
Cover art copyright © 1987 by George Tsui
Produced by Mega-Books of New York, Inc.

ISBN: 0-671-62652-3

First Minstrel Books printing October 1987

10 9 8 7 6 5 4

Printed in the U.S.A.

Contents

THE CASE OF
THE RUNAWAY
MONEY

1

"On Your Mark . . ."

Bang!

The starter's gun sounded. And the Lakeport Kids' Mini-Marathon to Help the Hungry started.

Twelve-year-old Nan Bobbsey and her twin, Bert, burst out of the pack and were immediately among the front runners.

"Hey!" shouted one of the other runners. "I lost my contact lens!"

Some racers began to slow down, including Nan. But her twin brother Bert grabbed her arm. "It's only Danny Rugg," he said. "Keep running!"

Nan picked up her pace. "He doesn't even wear contact lenses!" she complained.

"No," Bert said. "He's pulled that trick be-

1

fore. He just wants us to lose our concentration."

"What a creep!" Nan said. Anger gave her a sudden burst of speed.

"Hey, wait for me!" Bert shouted.

Nan glanced over her shoulder and grinned. Bert's long strides were quickly narrowing the gap.

All the other runners were off now. But Danny Rugg had gotten himself into the lead. Nan stared at him through the crowd. Danny was the school bully—and as his trick showed, he wasn't too honest.

Bert was alongside Nan now. She'd have to work to keep up with his pace.

Ahead of them was the one-mile marker. Only four more to go.

As Nan ran past the marker, she glanced over her shoulder. What had started out as a tight bunch of forty runners now looked like a parade. A string of kids stretched behind her on the road. Some looked as though they were ready to quit. Others kept pounding along, trying to catch up to the leaders.

She turned to look ahead. There were a lot less kids up that way.

Nan changed her breathing pattern. This wasn't the time to run out of breath—not even halfway to the finish.

She looked straight ahead and concentrated

on her pacing. Even so, her legs were beginning to ache a little.

Two Miles, said the next sign. The halfway mark would be coming up in a few minutes.

"Flossie . . . and Freddie," Nan called to Bert. She pointed to their brother and sister. The younger twins were standing by the road at the halfway station.

"Want a drink?" Freddie and Flossie both yelled. They darted onto the road, each holding a cup of water. As they ran beside Nan and Bert, the water in the cups sloshed up and down.

"Hey!" Nan said. "Leave some for us!"

"Go, Bert!" Flossie shouted, handing him her paper cup.

"Yeah, keep it up, Nan," Freddie cheered her on.

Nan took the cup from him, drank the water, then tossed the cup back to him, without breaking stride.

"We'll see you at the finish line!" Freddie called as the older twins pulled ahead.

"You're going to beat us there?" Bert called back.

"Yeah!" Freddie said with a grin. "You'll see!"

Bert didn't say anything more. He needed his breath to reach the three-mile marker.

Nan looked over her shoulder again. The

runners made a long, ragged line now. And they were getting tired. Even as she watched, one boy wobbled over to the side of the road. He sat down, rubbing his legs.

She knew just how the boy felt.

Up ahead was the four-mile marker. Nan tried to ignore how tired her legs felt. She concentrated on her pacing.

She and Bert were passing kids now. A lot of the kids had pushed themselves too early. Now they were all in.

Nan glanced at her brother. "One . . . more . . . mile!" she shouted. It was hard to get the words out.

Bert's eyes were on the road in front of them. Just eight runners were ahead.

The road curved, and Bert sped up for a second. "There's the winner's platform!" he wheezed.

"I see it," Nan puffed. A large crowd was bunched at the finish line. "We've got it made!"

"We'll be in the top ten!" Bert shouted.

Up ahead, the first runner crossed the finish line. But Nan didn't notice. She was watching the sidelines. "Look!" she said.

Freddie and Flossie were running along the side of the road. "Told you we'd beat you!" Freddie laughed.

"We cut through the park," Flossie cried.

Nan and Bert grinned. "Well, you haven't

beaten us yet!" They picked up speed, leaving Freddie and Flossie behind.

"Come on!" said Freddie to his twin. "I know a shortcut to the winner's platform." He ran toward some bushes.

Flossie followed him through the shrubs. "Slow down, Freddie," she said. "These bushes are scratching me."

Freddie ignored her and plunged through another bush. Then he stopped short. Flossie hit him from behind, nearly pushing him into a parked truck.

"Watch it!" Freddie yelled.

"It wasn't my fault," Flossie said. She looked at the truck. "Hey, isn't that Mr. Winters's armored truck?"

"Yes," Freddie said. He started around the truck. "I wonder what it's doing here?"

"It's *parked,* silly," Flossie said. She stopped at the end of the truck. "The back door is open," she said. "I've never seen the inside of an armored truck."

"Well, you can stand there and look." Freddie kicked at a little pile of blue paper that had caught on the wheel. "But I'm going to beat Nan and Bert." He started to run.

"Wait up!" Flossie yelled, running after him.

Bert had just crossed the finish line ahead of Nan when Freddie and Flossie ran up.

"Rats!" Freddie said when he saw them. Nan heard him and hid a grin.

"Come on, Nan," Bert said. "We need a cool-down lap."

"Good idea," she said, and took off.

They jogged around the winner's platform, listening to the cheers of the crowd as more and more kids finished the race.

When Nan and Bert got back to the finish line, Flossie and Freddie were waiting for them.

"The mayor's just about to announce the top ten finishers," Flossie said.

Mayor Childress grabbed the microphone set up on the winner's platform. He smiled down at the finish-line crowd and began calling out the names of the marathon's top finishers. After the eighth name, he said, "Bert and Nan Bobbsey."

While the crowd applauded, Nan and Bert climbed to the top of the winner's platform. They stood next to the other runners.

Danny Rugg grinned at them. "Well, if it isn't Nerd and Also-Ran Bobbsey."

Nan turned away. "I think he should be disqualified," she whispered to Bert.

Mayor Childress waited until the clapping died down. "Now I'd like to introduce the other members of the wonderful committee who ran the Lakeport Kids' Mini-Marathon to Help the Hungry."

He turned. "Starting on my left, there's Mrs. Cox, wife of City Councilman Cox. Jackson Winters, owner of Winters Armored Truck Service. He and his assistant, Hank Caldwell, have been very helpful. Then there's . . ." He stopped and placed his hand over the microphone.

"Where's Harrison Potter, the director of the Lakeport Cultural Events Office?" he asked Mrs. Cox.

"He called me this morning," she answered. "He had a family emergency in Cleveland."

The mayor nodded. "And let's thank Nan Bobbsey," he said, speaking into the microphone, "for making the wonderful treasure chest to hold the contributions."

Nan raised her hand as the clapping started again.

The mayor held up the treasure chest, a cardboard box covered in blue crepe paper. "And now," he said, "we've reached the moment everyone has been waiting for."

He patted the box. "Inside this treasure chest is money," said the mayor. "Some came in the mail, some was given in person by the good people of Lakeport. All of it is going to help the needy children in our community."

The mayor shook the box. "It's good and heavy," he joked. "I'm now going to open it, so we can all find out just how much money the marathon has raised."

The crowd buzzed with excitement.

Nan watched Mayor Childress tear open the treasure chest she had made. For a long moment he stood there, staring into the box, his mouth hanging open.

Then Mrs. Cox moved. She looked over the mayor's shoulder and her eyes widened. "The money!" she exclaimed.

"The money is . . . gone!"

2

Pennies from Heaven

A hush fell over the crowd. Hundreds of people stared as Mayor Childress reached into the box and pulled out a fistful of cut-up newspaper.

Nan glanced at the members of the marathon committee. They were glaring at each other.

"Who was watching that treasure chest?" asked Mayor Childress.

"I was," said Mrs. Cox.

"Who was watching *you?*" Jackson Winters demanded.

"What are you saying?" said Mrs. Cox.

Jackson Winters never got to answer. Hank Caldwell was asking a question, instead. "Where did you say Harrison Potter was?"

"Cleveland," answered Mrs. Cox.

Hank Caldwell frowned. "Cleveland, my foot. I bet Potter stole that money."

"Wait a minute," Bert said. "Let's not start accusing people. There has to be a logical answer for this."

"Let's go over where that box has been," Nan suggested. "Right from the start." The Bobbseys knew that a good detective always started at the beginning and went over all the facts.

Flossie zipped up the platform stairs with Freddie. "The first thing you did was make the treasure chest," Flossie said to Nan. "I helped."

"That's right," Nan said. "I decorated a cardboard box with blue crepe paper. Then I took it to Mr. Potter's office. That was two weeks ago."

"Okay," Freddie said. "What happened after that?"

"Well, I gave the chest to Mr. Potter and his secretary, Mary Rogers," Nan continued. "They had a special display table set up in their office. That way, people could either bring by their donations or mail them in."

"That's right," said Hank Caldwell. "I saw it when I made my donation."

"So how long did the box stay in that office?" Bert asked.

"Until Potter handed the chest over to me

yesterday," said Mayor Childress. "And my secretary and I locked it up in our safe."

"Then, this morning, you handed it over to
me." Mr. Winters took up the story. "My
driver, Hank, and I took it to this platform in
my armored truck."

"That's right," said Hank. "I never let that
treasure chest out of my sight. While Mr. Winters was driving the truck, I was locked up with
the chest in the back. There's no way anybody
could have stolen the money."

"Besides, the Lakeport High School Band
was marching in front of us," said Mr. Winters.
"They would have noticed anything suspicious."

"When we arrived," Hank continued, "I unlocked the truck door from inside. Then I
handed the treasure chest to Mrs. Cox."

"And I put it right here on this table," said
Mrs. Cox. *In full view of everybody!*"

"That treasure chest would have been torn up
if somebody tried to take the money out," Bert
said. "But it was sealed up tight."

"That's right," Nan said. "So somebody got
the money out without tearing the box open."

Freddie was puzzled. "But how?"

"Maybe it was magic," Flossie suggested.

Freddie rolled his eyes. Sometimes he
couldn't believe his twin sister.

Just then, Lieutenant Pike arrived in his patrol car. "Okay, folks," he said. "What's all this about some missing money?"

The mayor explained what had happened.

"This is almost like one of those locked-room mysteries, isn't it?" the lieutenant said.

"What's that?" Freddie asked.

"A crime that happens in a room that's locked from inside," Bert answered. "With no way in or out, how could anybody get inside to pull off the crime?"

"Right," said Lieutenant Pike. "In this case, the locked room is the treasure chest. There was no way in, without wrecking the box. But somehow, someone got the money out. And I'm going to find whoever it was."

"You can count on our help," Nan said.

"Now, listen, kids," said Lieutenant Pike. "I know you're good detectives. But this is a matter for the police. I don't want you getting involved in something that doesn't concern you."

"Doesn't concern us?" Nan said. "The marathon was our idea. I made that chest. We want to find the person who ruined it all."

"You know what I mean," the lieutenant said. "Police work is for the police."

Bert shrugged. "I guess then we should start heading for home," he said.

"Bert!" Nan said. She couldn't believe he was giving up so easily.

Bert started down the stairs, and the other Bobbseys followed. As soon as they were behind Lieutenant Pike, Bert winked at Nan.

She grinned. That meant they *weren't* going to give up the case.

"Where did Mom drop off our bikes?" asked Nan.

"Right here, behind the platform," Freddie said.

The twins found their bikes and pedaled off.

"I'm really mad about this whole thing," Nan said. They had stopped at a red light. "There are lots of needy kids in this town. Now they'll get nothing."

"I know," Bert said. "But Lieutenant Pike wasn't going to listen to us. We need to figure out what we're going to do. And the best place to make plans is at home."

"Right," agreed Freddie and Flossie.

"Hey, Mom!" Flossie called as soon as the twins arrived home.

"She's probably not back from picking up Dad at the airport," Nan said.

Bert looked at the clock on the kitchen wall. "What time did his flight get in?" he asked.

"Four o'clock," said Freddie.

15

Nan stuck her head into the living room. "Hi, Mrs. Green."

Their part-time housekeeper glanced away from the soap opera she was watching. "Your mother isn't home yet. She's out at the airport."

"Thanks," Nan said, looking over at the screen. "So, is Eddie going to marry Melissa?"

Mrs. Green shook her head. "I don't think so. Vance Tyrell is back in town."

"Uh-oh," Nan said, grinning.

She turned to Bert and the other twins. "Let's go up to my room," she said.

Bert led the way.

"I think we should make some notes," Nan was saying. She followed Bert into her room. Then she stopped. "What's that?" She pointed to her bed. Three dark blue envelopes were lying on top of it.

"They look like those special marathon envelopes," said Bert. "The ones people used to slip money into the treasure chest."

"But what are they doing on your bed?" Freddie wanted to know.

Nan shook her head. "I have no idea."

Flossie picked up an envelope and opened it. "Look," she said. "It has your name on it. And there's money inside."

"Let me see that." Nan almost jerked the envelope out of Flossie's hand.

"Hey, don't get mad at me," Flossie said. "*I* didn't do anything wrong." She gave Nan a funny look.

"Well, I didn't, either." Even as Nan spoke, she could feel her face turning scarlet.

"Nobody said you did," Bert said.

"Then what's all this?" Nan pointed to the other envelopes.

Freddie picked up the two envelopes and opened them. "More money," he said.

Everybody turned toward Nan.

"I don't get it," she said. "Somebody's trying to make it look like I stole that money."

"Why would anyone do that?" Bert asked.

The front doorbell rang.

"I'll get it," Flossie said.

"No, *I'll* get it." Nan rushed out of the room and down the stairs before Mrs. Green was off the couch.

When Nan opened the front door, she saw Hank Caldwell. He was holding the torn-up treasure chest in his hands.

"I thought you might like to have this," he said.

"I don't know what I'll do with it," Nan said. "But thanks for bringing it by."

"Actually, I didn't think you'd want it," said Hank. "I just wanted to come by and tell you I was sorry about what happened. I know how important this marathon was to you. Maybe I should just throw this box away, all right?"

"Okay," Nan said. "Thanks again for—" She stopped. Hank was staring at her hand.

Nan looked down. She was still clutching the blue envelope. And the money was sticking out, plain to see.

3

Lots of Suspects

"We're home," called Mr. Bobbsey, coming in the back door of the house.

Hank Caldwell looked at Nan. "Uh, well, I guess I'd better be going," he said.

"It—it's not what you think," Nan said.

"I can hear Nan's voice." Mrs. Bobbsey was walking through the kitchen. "Nan, where are you?"

Nan turned. "I'm at the front door," she said. When she turned back, Hank Caldwell was gone.

Mrs. Bobbsey came into the front hallway. "What's the matter, sweetheart?" She could see how upset Nan was.

Nan held out the blue envelope. "This," she said.

"Is that one of those I put on your bed this morning?" asked Mrs. Bobbsey.

Nan stared at her mother. "What?" she said. "*You* put it on my bed?"

"They were in the mailbox when I checked the mail this morning," said Mrs. Bobbsey. "You had already left for the marathon. I thought you'd know what to do with them."

"I know what they are," Nan said. "But I don't know why anybody would put them in our mailbox, unless . . ."

"Unless what?" said Mrs. Bobbsey.

"Hey, there!" Mr. Bobbsey stood in the entrance to the living room. Nan ran over and gave him a hug.

"Welcome back, Dad," she said.

"Thanks, sweetheart," said Mr. Bobbsey. "Now, what are we talking about that needs explaining?" He looked from Nan to Mrs. Bobbsey, then back to Nan.

"Come up to my room," Nan said. "At least part of this puzzle has been solved."

As the three of them started up the stairs, they saw Bert, Freddie, and Flossie at the top. "Mom! Dad! Hi!" The kids rushed down to hug their parents.

They finally reached Nan's room, where Nan pointed to the other blue envelopes on the bed. "Mom, will you tell everyone where these came from?"

Mrs. Bobbsey explained about finding the envelopes in the mailbox.

"Nan thinks somebody's trying to frame her," Freddie said.

"What?" said Mrs. Bobbsey.

"What are you talking about, Freddie?" said Mr. Bobbsey.

"I'll explain," Nan said. She told her parents about the money stolen from the treasure chest. "Then this money turns up here." She sighed. "And at least one person thinks *I* stole the money. He saw me with this." She held up the envelope with the money sticking out. "Hank probably thinks I was counting my loot."

"Hank who?" Bert asked.

"Hank Caldwell," Nan answered. "That's who was at the door. I know he saw the envelope in my hand."

"What did he come by for?" Bert asked.

"Just to say he was sorry for what had happened," Nan said.

"He's probably on his way to the police station right now," Freddie said. "You'd better leave town, Nan."

"Thanks a lot, Freddie!" Nan gave him a look.

Freddie grinned. "Just trying to save your life."

"Well, *we* all know that Nan wouldn't take

the money," said Mr. Bobbsey. "And we can prove she didn't. So the matter is settled."

"I bet the person who put those envelopes in the mailbox is the same person who stole the marathon money." Nan frowned.

"I wonder who it was," Flossie said.

"I have *my* suspect," Bert said.

"Who is it?" Freddie asked.

"Jackson Winters."

"I think we should leave," said Mrs. Bobbsey, "before *we* get on their suspect list."

"Oh, Mom," Flossie said. "You couldn't have stolen the money. You were at the airport, picking up Dad."

"Well, I like that!" said Mrs. Bobbsey. "Is that the only reason you think I couldn't have done it?"

"Wellllllll . . ." Flossie pretended to think for a moment. Then the twins and their parents began laughing.

"Dinner will be ready in about an hour," Mrs. Bobbsey said. "I'll call you."

"Okay," said the twins.

"But first," said Mrs. Bobbsey, "I'll have to pry Mrs. Green away from the television."

"That won't be easy," Nan called out as her parents headed down the stairs. "*Another Turning World* is on."

She turned to Bert. "Okay. Now tell us

why you think Mr. Winters is guilty."

"Mr. Winters wouldn't hurt anyone," Flossie said.

"Do you remember that armored truck robbery a couple of years ago?" Bert asked.

"I remember," Freddie said. "Police cars racing all over the place . . ."

"Well, what about it?" Nan asked.

"There was some talk that Mr. Winters robbed his own truck," Bert said.

"I thought he got hit over the head," Freddie said.

"Oh, he had marks," Bert said. "But he could have faked being hit—done it to himself. Then it would look like somebody else did the robbing."

"I'll bet that hurts," Flossie said. "I could never do that to myself."

"I wouldn't put it past Mr. Winters," Nan said. "He'd probably do anything for money. He's such a miser."

"What's a miser?" Flossie asked.

"Somebody who keeps all his money and never spends any," Nan said.

"You mean like Freddie?" Flossie said.

Freddie made a face as the other twins laughed. "That is Mr. Winters, all right," he had to admit.

"Well, I like him," Flossie said. "He's always been nice to me."

"Who do you think stole the money, then?" Freddie asked.

"Mrs. Cox." Flossie nodded her head and folded her arms.

"Why Mrs. Cox?" Nan asked.

"I always thought she was okay," Bert said.

"She's not nice," Flossie said. "She's a horse-hater."

"What does hating horses have to do with stealing money?" Bert was confused.

"It shows how mean she is," Flossie replied.

"Okay, Flossie"—Nan sighed—"tell us about it."

"Mrs. Cox was the one who closed the riding paths in Lakeport State Park," Flossie said.

"And?" Nan said.

"And anyone who would do that is really bad," Flossie finished.

"I don't think Mrs. Cox stole the money," Freddie said. "It was Mayor Childress."

"You're kidding," Nan said. "The mayor?"

"You know that empty lot downtown?" Freddie asked.

The twins nodded.

"The mayor had all the weeds cut down. Then he turned it into a parking lot."

"Downtown needed more parking," Nan said. "That was a good idea."

"I don't think it was a good idea," Freddie said. "He ruined that lot! It was the best place

25

around here to catch bugs for my collection."

"Yuck!" Flossie said.

"Come on, Freddie," Bert said. "That vacant lot was a health hazard."

"Maybe," Freddie said. "But it had a lot of bugs."

"That's silly," Flossie said. "My suspect is better than yours."

"Your suspect is stupid," Freddie answered.

Bert turned to Nan. "Who's your suspect?" he asked, before the younger twins got into a fight.

"I go with Harrison Potter," Nan said. "I've never told anyone this before. But I think he was jealous because the marathon was my idea. I think he wanted it to fall through."

"That's *really* mean," Flossie said.

"He had the treasure chest the longest," Nan went on. "And he was the only one who didn't show up today. That looks awfully suspicious to me."

Bert stood up. "We sure have a lot of suspects," he said. "I can't wait to investigate them!"

"Let's go!" Flossie and Freddie said together.

"Dinner's ready," called Mrs. Bobbsey.

"Tomorrow," Nan said, laughing.

4

The Shopping Spree

The next day, Flossie ran down the street to Drummond's Department Store. She pushed through the revolving doors. Bert followed.

"Come on, Bert," Flossie said. "Mrs. Cox will be gone if we don't hurry."

"How do you know she's even here?" Bert asked.

"I called her home," Flossie said. "Her housekeeper said she'd gone to Drummond's. They're having a fur sale. This will be a great place to tail her. You'll see. I bet we'll even get some evidence."

They took the escalator to the third floor. When they got off, they headed for a sign that said Fur Department.

"She must be around here somewhere," Flossie said.

"What do you plan to do when you find her?" Bert asked.

Flossie stopped in her tracks. "I don't know."

"It's a good thing I'm along, then," Bert said. "I know just what to do. Rex Sleuther had a case like this in last month's issue." Bert was Lakeport's biggest fan of *Rex Sleuther* comics. "You can be my assistant," he told Flossie. "We have to get close without being seen."

They turned left and found themselves in the fur department. Flossie almost ran into Mrs. Cox, who was taking off a mink coat and shaking her head.

"Quick," Flossie whispered, "let's hide inside one of these coats."

She grabbed Bert and pulled him inside a dark fur coat. Bert could see the price tag dangling in front of him—$10,000.

"You look through one sleeve and I'll look through the other," Flossie said. "We'll be able to see what she's doing."

The sleeves of the fur coat began moving around like periscopes.

"Now here is something you should try on," said the saleswoman. "This fox jacket just came in this morning. It's definitely your color." She helped Mrs. Cox slip into the fur.

"It does have a wonderful feel to it," said Mrs. Cox. "How much does it cost?"

"It's a steal at only five thousand dollars," said the saleswoman.

Flossie gasped. "Did you hear that?" she whispered to Bert.

"I'm getting hot in here, Flossie," Bert whispered back.

"I'll take it," said Mrs. Cox. "Have it sent to my home."

"Would you like to charge it?" the saleswoman asked.

"I always pay cash," said Mrs. Cox.

"Did you hear *that*, Bert?" Flossie's voice got more and more excited.

They peered through the sleeves of the dark coat. Mrs. Cox counted out a big stack of bills.

"That's all the proof we need," Flossie said. "She stole the money. Now she's using it to buy herself a fur jacket."

"Hmmmm," Bert said. "It sure looks that way."

"The poor kids in this town will be freezing this winter." Flossie's voice was angry. "But she'll be warm and cozy in that fur! I think we should arrest her."

"We can't arrest anybody, Flossie," Bert said. "We can only collect evidence."

"We *have* evidence," Flossie said.

"Not enough," Bert said. "Rex Sleuther would keep tailing her."

"Will there be anything else, Mrs. Cox?" the saleswoman asked.

"Perhaps some shoes," said Mrs. Cox.

"That department is on our second floor."

"I know," said Mrs. Cox. "Thank you." She picked up her receipt and headed toward the escalator.

"Come on," Bert said, stepping out of the fur coat. "After her!"

But Flossie didn't appear. "Can't get . . . out!" Her voice was muffled by the heavy coat. "I'm stuck!"

"Don't pull too hard," Bert said. "You'll rip the sleeve."

Flossie began tugging gently, but she couldn't get free. The coat began to shake wildly as she struggled. "Bert, what am I going to do?" she said.

"Here," Bert whispered, "let me try." He stepped back inside the coat and tried to free Flossie.

"May I help you?"

Flossie and Bert both peeked out of the fur coat.

The saleswoman who had waited on Mrs. Cox was looking at them. "Are you interested in buying that coat?" she asked.

"I might be," Flossie said. "I was just trying it on for size."

"These are adult sizes, young lady." The saleswoman arched an eyebrow. "And we don't have this style in your size."

Flossie gave a desperate tug and pulled herself free of the coat. "In that case, I guess we won't buy it. Come on, Bert. We'll just have to spend our money someplace else."

"Fine with me," Bert said. He took Flossie's hand. Flossie tilted up her nose.

They walked to the escalator as quickly as they could. And they didn't look back.

Bert and Flossie got off the escalator at the second floor and headed for the shoe department.

"There's Mrs. Cox," Bert said.

"Oh, good," Flossie said. "I'll just pretend to look at these red sandals here."

"The little girls' shoes are on the other side," said a voice. "And the boys' shoes are on the other side of that."

Flossie and Bert looked up. A man was standing beside them.

"Actually, we're looking for shoes for our mother," Flossie said.

"That's different," said the man. "What size does she wear?"

Flossie looked desperately at Bert. "Um—we're not sure," he said.

"But I'm sure I'll recognize it when I see it," Flossie added.

The man looked confused. "Don't you think it would be better to find out the right size?"

From the corner of her eye, Flossie could see Mrs. Cox. She was trying on shoes, with lots of boxes around her. "No," Flossie said.

"It's her birthday today," Bert said, thinking quickly. "We want to surprise her."

Flossie grinned. "And there's no time to find out what size she wears," she added.

Mrs. Cox stood up and headed for the cash register. A salesman followed with several shoeboxes.

"Does this look like your mother's size?" the man asked Flossie. He held out a pair of shoes.

"Now that I see them up close," Flossie said, "I don't think she'd like those shoes."

"I still say we should get her a nice scarf," Bert said.

The man put the shoes down. "Kids!" he said.

Flossie took Bert's arm. She steered him over to where Mrs. Cox was standing. When they were close enough to hear, Flossie ducked behind a shoe display. She pulled Bert down with her.

"Will that be cash or charge?" asked the salesman.

"I always pay in cash," said Mrs. Cox.

"Sure, you do," Flossie whispered. "Especially when you've just stolen a lot of money from poor kids!"

"Shhhh!" Bert hissed. "You can't keep talking when you're tailing a suspect."

The salesman rang up Mrs. Cox's bill. "That will be five hundred dollars," he said.

"Five hundred plus five thousand," Bert said. "That's a lot of money!"

"I can't believe it," Flossie said. "That woman is spending all the marathon money on herself. Let's get closer."

"No," Bert said. "I think we've collected enough evidence on Mrs. Cox. Let's go home."

"I guess you believe me now," Flossie said. "Mrs. Cox stole that money. And we've got enough evidence to lock her up!"

5

You Can't Fight City Hall

Bert and Flossie burst through the kitchen door. They found Freddie eating pizza and Nan reading a book.

"We've solved the mystery!" Flossie announced.

Freddie jumped. The cheese slid right off his pizza. "I don't believe it," he said.

"It's true," Flossie said. "I told you it was Mrs. Cox."

"You mean Mrs. Cox stole the marathon money?" Freddie tried to scoop up his cheese.

"How do you know?" Nan asked. "Did she walk up to you and confess?"

"No," Bert said. "But she was acting very suspiciously."

Mrs. Bobbsey came into the kitchen. "Where have you two been?" she asked.

"Bert and I tailed Mrs. Cox in Drummond's Department Store," Flossie said. "She was spending all the money she stole from the treasure chest."

"What's this?" asked Mrs. Bobbsey. She looked at Bert.

"She bought a fur coat and a lot of shoes," he said. "You should have seen all the cash she had."

"Oh," said Mrs. Bobbsey. "Well, you can forget about Mrs. Cox. She's not your thief."

The twins looked at Mrs. Bobbsey.

"Why not, Mom?" Nan asked. "That does sound suspicious."

"Yeah," Flossie said. "We have to call Lieutenant Pike and turn her in."

"Hold it," said Mrs. Bobbsey. "There's something you need to know about the Cox family."

"What?" Freddie asked.

"Your grandfather told me this story," said Mrs. Bobbsey. "Years ago, the Cox family lost a lot of money in a bank failure. It was only a small part of their fortune, but still, it was a great deal of money to lose. They vowed never again to trust banks. Instead, they keep their money at home in a safe. And they pay for everything in cash."

"Weird," Nan said.

"Not too smart, either," Bert said.

Mrs. Bobbsey shrugged. "I agree, but that's what they do. They never charge or write a check for anything. Mrs. Cox wasn't doing anything strange for her."

"I thought I'd solved the mystery." Flossie was disappointed.

"Don't worry about it, Floss," Bert said. "We won't give up."

Flossie smiled.

"I'll tell you one thing about this case," said Mrs. Bobbsey. "You're talking about some of the most important people in town. Before you go to Lieutenant Pike, you'd better be *very* sure. And you'd better have real proof."

Nan set her book down. "You're right, Mom," she said. Then she turned to the other twins. "Let's go to my room and see where we are now."

Freddie stuffed the last bit of pizza into his mouth and ran after the others.

They sat down on the floor in Nan's room.

"Looks like we'll have to scratch Mrs. Cox from the list of suspects," Nan said. She looked at Freddie. "What do you have to report about the mayor?"

"Nothing yet," Freddie answered. "But to-morrow I'll have this thing solved."

"Oh, really?" Bert said.

"Yep." Freddie smiled. "Our class is taking a field trip to City Hall. We're going to visit the mayor's office."

"I forgot about that," Flossie said. "Maybe I can help you, Freddie."

"You can help me a lot," Freddie said. "Just stay out of my way."

Flossie stuck out her tongue. "I bet they made a mistake at the hospital," she said. "I bet my *real* twin brother is nice."

The next morning, the school bus with Freddie and Flossie's class arrived at City Hall. The class was met on the steps by the mayor himself.

"Welcome, welcome," said Mayor Childress. "It's wonderful that young people like you are getting to see democracy in action. We're going to spend the morning finding out how a city works. Let's go to the water department first."

Mrs. Hanson, their teacher, followed the mayor. The class marched after Mrs. Hanson. Freddie and Flossie brought up the rear.

"I just know the mayor's the one who stole that charity money," Freddie said.

"How do you know?" Flossie asked.

"Crooks talk the same way the mayor talks," Freddie answered. "You hear them all the time on TV."

"They do?" Flossie said.

"Flossie! Freddie!" called Mrs. Hanson. "No talking in line, please. Pay attention to what the mayor is saying."

"Yes, Mrs. Hanson," they both said.

They had arrived at the water department. A man showed them a map of all the water lines in the city of Lakeport.

"Here are all the water towers," the man said. "And here are all the pipes the water runs through."

Flossie yawned. "This is boring," she whispered to Freddie.

But Freddie was twisting in his seat, looking around. "Where did the mayor go?"

"I think he went down those stairs." Flossie pointed behind them.

"This is my chance," Freddie said. "I'm going to follow the mayor. I'll bet he's going to wherever he hid the marathon money."

"Better not leave, Freddie," Flossie warned. "You'll get in trouble."

"How can I get in trouble if I catch a crook?" Freddie asked.

"Oh, okay," Flossie said. "But hurry up."

"This way, class," said Mrs. Hanson. "We're visiting the city planner's office next."

"You go on," Freddie whispered to Flossie. "I'll just sort of hang back until you get around the corner. Mrs. Hanson said we'd be here for an hour." He checked his watch. "That gives me about thirty minutes. I'll catch up to you."

"I hope so," Flossie said. "Be careful."

Freddie grinned. "Don't worry. I'll be fine."

The class had already disappeared around the corner. Flossie hurried to join them.

Freddie headed for the staircase. A sign on the wall said: To Basement. He ran down the stairs.

Cautiously opening the fire door, he peeked around. In the dim basement, he heard a noise. It sounded like the engine of a car. Yes, it had to be. Freddie could smell exhaust fumes. Then the engine died. Silence.

Freddie stepped into the basement, leaving the fire door open behind him.

The basement was dark—except for a small area to his left. There, a floodlight lit up a sleek red sports car. The car looked very expensive. And by the car, wearing coveralls, was the mayor, looking under the hood.

I knew it, Freddie thought. He *did* steal the marathon money. And he bought an expensive sports car with it. What a greedy person.

Freddie crept closer. Then he froze. The mayor shut the hood with a bang. He watched the mayor get inside the car and start the engine. It revved a couple of times, then stopped. Mayor Childress got out and raised the hood again.

I've got him red-handed, Freddie thought.

A sound came from behind him.

Grrrrrrrr.

Or he's got me. Freddie turned slowly. He found himself staring at the face of a German shepherd. "Nice boy," he whispered.

Grrrrrrrrrrrrrr. The dog growled louder. Then it barked three times.

"What's wrong, Fritz?" called the mayor. "Found a cat?"

I wish, Freddie thought.

Grrrrrrrrrrrrrrrrrrrr!

A couple of boxes stood between Fritz and Freddie. About twenty feet behind Freddie was the fire door he'd come through. If he pushed over some of the boxes, he'd distract Fritz. Maybe the boxes would even block the dog while Freddie ran for the door.

Of course, the mayor would know someone had been in the basement. But he wouldn't know who. The important thing was getting out—alive.

Freddie took a deep breath. Then he shoved at the boxes with all his might.

When the boxes went tumbling, they startled Fritz—for a second.

Freddie raced for the door. There would be no time to push it shut. The dog was right behind him—and getting closer!

6

Locked Up

Freddie reached the door. The dog had almost caught him when the mayor shouted, "Fritz!"

That made the big German shepherd freeze. "You get back here this instant."

Freddie leaned against the wall. He could hear Fritz padding back to the mayor. Then he looked at his watch. Time was running out. He needed to find his class.

On the first floor, Freddie found the city planner's office. He asked the receptionist where Mrs. Hanson's class was.

"They're probably in the mayor's office by now," said the receptionist. "That was the last place they were going."

"The mayor's office?" Freddie said. "Where's that?"

"Third floor," the receptionist said. Freddie raced up the stairs. He arrived just as the last members of the class filed into the office.

"Hurry up, Freddie," said Mrs. Hanson. "The mayor is going to talk to us before we go back to school."

That'll be a neat trick, thought Freddie. He walked into the office, which was filled with folding chairs. Luckily, the one behind Flossie was empty.

"What took you so long?" Flossie asked. "I was getting worried. What if Mrs. Hanson had asked me where you were?"

"I've solved the mystery," Freddie said. "The mayor did it. I saw him down in the basement. He was working on a fancy sports car. What do you bet he bought it with the stolen money?"

Flossie stared at him. "Are you—" she began. Then a door opened at the side of the mayor's office. And the mayor stepped into the room. He no longer had his coveralls on.

Flossie's and Freddie's mouths dropped open. Then Freddie understood. "It's an elevator," he whispered to Flossie. "A private elevator!"

"Hello, again, boys and girls," said Mayor Childress. He walked to his desk and sat down on the edge. "Have you seen how this great city of ours works?"

"Yes," the class answered.

"Wonderful!" said the mayor. "But you should always remember, there's more to life than work." He held up his hands. "Do you know why my hands are so dirty?"

"No," cried the class.

"I do," Freddie whispered.

The mayor smiled. "I was down in the basement, working on my sports car."

"Oooooooooh," the class exclaimed.

"I've been working on it for the past year," the mayor continued. "I cut my lunch hour short. Then I use those few extra minutes to go down and tinker with that automobile. It's my dream to race in this year's Lakeport Grand Prix."

The class *ooooooh*ed again.

Freddie looked at Flossie.

"You can work hard, boys and girls—and still have fun." Mayor Childress stood up. "That's the message I want to leave with you. Have a safe trip back to school."

Mrs. Hanson and the class applauded.

Freddie and Flossie clapped, too. But their hearts weren't in it.

On the bus back to school, the kids all chattered about what they'd seen. But Freddie sat glumly in the back of the bus.

"He's been working on that sports car for a year. That means he didn't buy it with the marathon money."

"Too bad," Flossie said. "I thought we'd caught the thief."

That afternoon, Freddie and Flossie waited for Nan and Bert on the front porch.

"Did the mayor steal the money?" Nan asked, parking her bike. Bert got off his, too.

Freddie shook his head. He told Nan and Bert what had happened. But he left out the part about Fritz. That was just *too* embarrassing.

The twins went inside.

"Looks like the mayor's dropped to the bottom of the list with Mrs. Cox," Bert said. He looked at Nan. "What are you doing about Harrison Potter?"

"Nothing much," Nan said. "Ms. Rogers, his secretary, says he's still in Cleveland. But he's supposed to be back soon." She turned to Bert. "How about your suspect?"

"I've got an interesting assignment in social studies," Bert said. "I have to write a report about how a business works. At first I was going to do Dad's lumber business—"

Freddie poked Flossie. "That sounds *real* interesting," he said.

Bert ignored him. "But now I'll talk to Mr. Winters. Maybe I can help out at his armored truck company. Spend a couple of days after school. And"—he grinned—"check around for the missing money."

"Great idea!" Nan said.

"Can I be your assistant again?" Flossie asked.

Bert shook his head. "This time, I'll have to work alone."

Disappointed, Flossie flopped into a chair.

Bert looked at his watch. "It's only four-thirty," he said. "Mr. Winters is probably still at his office. I think I'll go see him now."

Bert went back outside and got on his bicycle. Minutes later, he arrived at Winters Armored Truck Service.

Hank Caldwell was sitting at the front desk.

"Hi," said Hank. "What brings you here?"

Bert explained about his school project. "Do you think Mr. Winters could help me out?" he asked.

Hank shrugged. "Don't really know. What would you want to know?" he asked.

"How about the armored car?" Bert said. "What kind of protection does it have? How is it built?"

"Look, this is Mr. Winters's business." Hank pointed with his thumb to the rear. "You'll have to ask him."

Bert went to Mr. Winters's office and knocked on the open door.

Mr. Winters looked up at Bert. "What do you want, son?" he asked. He was standing by a filing cabinet, looking at papers.

Bert told Mr. Winters about his report.

"I don't know," said Mr. Winters. "I'm not used to having kids around. But if you really want to know about this business, ask Hank. He'll show you around."

"Thanks, Mr. Winters." Bert dashed back to the front office. When he told Hank what Mr. Winters had said, Hank frowned. "Where do you want to start?" he asked.

"Well, I've never seen the inside of an armored truck," Bert said.

"That's the idea," Hank said. "We're *supposed* to keep people out." He shrugged. "But come on."

Bert followed Hank through a side door into the garage. An armored truck was parked inside. Hank pulled open the door of the cab.

Bert looked around. "Just like a regular truck," he said. "Except for this."

He pointed at the back of the cab. Instead of a window, there was a steel panel.

Hank rapped on the steel. "This is how the driver talks to whoever's in back," he said.

Bert blinked. "You mean the driver has to open that, just to talk?"

"The driver can't open it. Only the person in the back. Say I was riding in the back, and Mr. Winters was driving. If he wanted to talk to me, he'd rap on the door. Then I'd slide it open."

Hank smiled at Bert's puzzlement. "It's security, son. Once I lock myself in the truck, *nobody* can get to me. When we get where we're going, I unlock the back door. But only if Mr. Winters tells me it's okay."

"And you were locked inside the other day with the treasure chest." Bert knocked on the steel with his knuckles.

"Yeah," said Hank. "That's how I know nothing happened to it."

Bert scratched his chin. "This is really interesting," he said. "Could I see the back of the truck, where you ride?"

Hank shrugged. "Not much to see," he said. He pulled a key from his pocket and unlocked the back door.

"It's heavy." Hank grunted as he pulled on the handle and opened the door.

Bert climbed up. "Not bad," he said, looking around. "It even has a carpet."

Hank Caldwell didn't answer. He quickly bent over and snatched something caught in a corner. "Nobody cleans up around here," he grumbled. "People should take care of things."

Bert couldn't see what Hank picked up. He only caught a flash of color—blue.

Hank put whatever it was in his pocket. Then he looked at his watch. "Closing time," he said.

"Could I come back tomorrow?" Bert asked. "I'd like to talk some more."

Hank shook his head. "We'll be busy tomorrow. Lots of shipments to pick up."

"If it's after school, maybe I could go along," Bert said. "Mr. Winters said I could help out."

"Not that way," Hank said. "We carry a lot of money. Sometimes it gets dangerous—and it's no place for a kid."

Bert stepped out of the truck. "So when *can* I come back? My report's due in two weeks."

"It's gonna be pretty busy around here," Hank said. "Let me call you when there's a good time."

Bert wrote down his phone number on a piece of paper. "Don't forget," he said. "I want to get a good grade."

Hank took the paper. "Sure, kid. See you around." He opened the garage door, and hustled Bert out.

Outside, Bert turned back. He saw Hank pull out the scrap he'd hidden in his pocket. Hank looked at it, then stared at Mr. Winters's office window.

Bert saw another flash of blue just before Hank headed back inside the garage. Then came a heavy *chunk!* as Hank slammed the truck's back door.

7
Whodunit?

When Bert got home, he found the other twins sitting in Nan's room. "Ms. Rogers called," Nan said. "I have an appointment with Harrison Potter tomorrow after school."

"Great," Bert said. "But you'll be wasting your time. Wait till you hear what I found out."

Flossie and Freddie looked up eagerly.

"Did Mr. Winters steal the money?" Flossie asked.

"I don't have any proof yet," Bert said. "But I think Hank Caldwell is covering something up."

He explained how Hank had picked up the blue scrap, then hidden it. "He was really upset after finding that scrap," Bert said. "Hank got

53

rid of me quick after that. Then he stood looking at *Mr. Winters's window!*"

"You think he suspects Mr. Winters of stealing the money?" Nan said.

Freddie nodded. "That makes sense."

"But how?" Nan asked. "Hank told us the
chest was locked with him in the truck."

"That's what Hank *says*," Bert said. "But Mr.
Winters is his boss. What if he stopped the
truck and made Hank open the doors? He could
have taken the box."

Nan shook her head. "That doesn't work.
The Lakeport High School Band was marching
in front of the truck. They'd have seen it stop."

Bert snapped his fingers. "He didn't have to
stop or get out! There's a sliding door from the
cab to the back. Suppose Mr. Winters made
Hank open it, and took the chest. He could
have stolen the money, then passed the box
back again."

Freddie jumped up and down. "And Hank is
afraid to say anything! He'll lose his job!"

"Poor Hank," Flossie said.

"Poor us," Bert said. "I just remembered that
the door in the truck is too small for the chest
to fit through."

"So Mr. Winters didn't steal the money?"

"I didn't say that, Freddie," Bert said. "Mr.
Winters is definitely up to something. But I'm

going to keep an eye on him—*and* his truck. Maybe I'll see him slip up."

"I still want to see how Mr. Potter acts," Nan said. "Especially when I tell him that I think he stole the money."

"You're crazy," Freddie said.

"Can I go with you?" Flossie asked.

"I'd love to have the company," Nan said. "But I'd feel better if I knew you were at home."

"Right," Flossie said. "That way, I can call the cops when Mr. Potter tries something."

"Flossie!" Bert said.

"That's the way it always happens on TV," Flossie answered.

The next afternoon, Nan parked her bicycle in front of City Hall. She bounded up the stairs to Harrison Potter's office.

Mary Rogers, Mr. Potter's secretary, looked up from the letter she was typing. "Oh, hello, Nan," she said.

"Hi," Nan said. "I made it right on time."

"Mr. Potter's still in the building," said Ms. Rogers. "But he's not in his office right now. He should be back in a few minutes."

"Could I just go inside and wait for him?" Nan asked. Here was a chance to look for clues.

"I guess that would be all right," said Ms.

Rogers. "I think you spent more time up here during the marathon drive than you did at home."

Nan grinned. She stepped toward Mr. Potter's office.

But Ms. Rogers grabbed her arm. "I'm so sorry about that stolen money. How could it have disappeared?"

"I have an idea," Nan said. "But it's nothing definite."

"It's a mystery to me," said Ms. Rogers. "Mr. Potter and I locked that treasure chest in the safe every night. Right up to the day we gave it to Mayor Childress."

Nan looked at Ms. Rogers. Was she lying? Nan didn't think so. "I'll go on inside and sit down," she said.

"Fine," said Ms. Rogers. "I have work to do."

Nan went into the office. She stood in the middle of the room, looking around. If I had that money, where would I hide it? she wondered. Mr. Potter had to have it around here. He *must* be the one who had stolen the money.

Nan turned and tiptoed around the desk. She pulled open a drawer. Inside were stationery and envelopes. She shut that drawer and opened another one.

"Poor Mr. Potter," Ms. Rogers called.

Startled, Nan shut the drawer on her finger. "Ouch!" She caught her breath and walked over to the door.

"What do you mean?" she asked.

"It's just been one disaster after another for him." Ms. Rogers shook her head. "Before this robbery, he had to rush over to Cleveland. His aunt was sick again. It's a terrible problem. Her treatment is so expensive, and she has no money."

Nan stepped out of the office. "So Mr. Potter has been helping her?"

"He's been helping her for years. But most of his money is tied up right now."

"How do you know that?" Nan asked.

"I hear him on the telephone, all the time," said Ms. Rogers. "He's desperately trying to raise the money for his aunt. I don't know how he'll do it."

I know how he did it, Nan thought. "That's too bad," she said.

"I have to step down the hall for a moment," said Ms. Rogers. "I'll be right back."

"Okay," Nan said. She darted back into Mr. Potter's office.

So, Mr. Potter has a motive for stealing the money, she thought. He disappeared the day the money did. I bet he took it to Cleveland for his aunt.

Nan sighed. It was too bad that Mr. Potter's

aunt needed help. Still, he had no right to give her the marathon money.

Nan looked around the office. Where could she find proof that Mr. Potter had stolen the money?

She walked over to a filing cabinet. Maybe she would find some of the blue charity envelopes in there. Maybe she'd even find some of the money.

The drawer slid open easily. Nan bent over, reading the papers inside.

She never heard the door opening behind her. She didn't know she was no longer alone until she heard the angry voice demanding, "What are you doing there?"

8
Coming Up Empty

Nan whirled around. She stared up at the angry face of Harrison Potter.

"I said, what are you doing?" he repeated.

"I—I was just looking," Nan stammered.

"For what?"

Then Nan remembered her plan. She took a deep breath. "I was looking for evidence," she said.

Mr. Potter loomed over her. "Evidence of what?"

But Nan stood her ground. "Evidence that you stole the marathon money."

Mr. Potter didn't answer Nan's charge. He simply stared at her.

"I know you have a sick aunt in Cleveland. And you've been taking care of her," Nan said.

Mr. Potter blinked. "What has my aunt got to do with this?"

"She has no money. And it costs a lot to take care of her," Nan said. "So . . ."

". . . So you think that's why I stole the marathon money?" Mr. Potter looked as if he couldn't decide whether to explode or laugh.

"Um . . . yes." All of a sudden, Nan didn't feel so sure.

Mr. Potter drummed his fingers on top of the file cabinet. "You had no business looking through my papers."

"I had to solve the crime," Nan said.

"Well, you haven't," snapped Mr. Potter. "I did *not* steal that money. Yes, the treatment for my aunt is expensive. I guess you heard that from Mary—Ms. Rogers."

He looked over at the door. "What you haven't heard is that I sold some stocks today. That will more than take care of Aunt Eloise. I didn't need to steal the money."

Nan's mind raced. Was Mr. Potter lying? "But it *has* to be you," she said. "Everything fits. You had a motive. And you disappeared the same day the money did . . . And . . ."

"And what?" said Mr. Potter.

"And I thought you were jealous about the marathon." Nan looked away. "Because it was my idea, and because it was such a success."

Mr. Potter sank down in his chair. He

breathed hard for a moment. "I guess you hadn't snooped your way into my desk yet."

"I wasn't *snooping*," Nan said. "I was searching for evidence."

"Then keep searching." Mr. Potter stepped away from his desk. "Be my guest."

Nan felt really stupid, going through the desk with Mr. Potter there. But she carefully checked each drawer. No blue envelopes. No charity money. Nothing. She could feel his eyes, boring into the top of her head.

"Don't forget the drawer in the middle," he said.

She pulled out the drawer. It held some worn-out pencils, a pen—and a sheet of paper.

Nan read the first few lines. Then she turned bright red. "Oh, no."

"Oh, yes," said Mr. Potter. "That letter was going out to the *Lakeport News* today. I was proud of the marathon. I wanted the whole town to know about the fine job you did, putting it together."

"Oh, Mr. Potter," Nan said. "I feel like such a jerk. And I was so sure . . ." She sighed. "I don't know what to say."

Mr. Potter just shrugged.

"At least let me apologize," Nan said. "I'm sorry for snooping around your office."

"Searching," said Mr. Potter with a little smile. "Apology accepted." He looked at his watch. "Time to go home. I'll see you out," he added.

But he stopped on his way to the door. "Why pick on me?" he asked, curious.

"You left town on the day of the theft," Nan said. "That looked very suspicious. Besides, you were the only suspect we had left."

Mr. Potter's eyebrows went up. "You had other suspects?"

"We checked all the other committee members," Nan explained. "But we've cleared them so far."

"You've been investigating *all* of us?" said Mr. Potter.

"Somebody ruined that marathon," Nan said. "Not just for me, but for all the needy kids in Lakeport. My brothers and my sister and I, we've promised we're going to find who did it."

"Looks as though you've come up empty," said Mr. Potter. "You said I was the last suspect."

"You are," Nan said sadly, "at least as far as I'm concerned. My brother Bert still has one left. But I think he's wrong."

"Look," said Mr. Potter, "maybe I shouldn't have been so rough on you. I know how hard you worked and how disappointed you must be. That's why I wrote that letter. You deserve a lot of praise."

"Thanks," Nan said softly.

"I've had a chance to calm down now," Mr. Potter said. "Maybe I'll send the letter after all."

Nan gave him the ghost of a smile.

Mr. Potter opened the door. "And, Nan," he said.

She turned in the doorway.

"Good luck."

Nan came in the front door. Flossie was lying on the living room floor, playing a video game. "Was Mr. Potter the crook?" she asked.

"No," Nan said. "He couldn't be."

"I still bet it's Mrs. Cox," Flossie insisted. "I probably missed a clue in the department store."

"We're *all* missing a clue," Nan said. "Come on, let's get the guys and go outside. I want to figure this thing out."

The twins all sat under a tree in the backyard. "I'm taking Harrison Potter off our suspect list," Nan said. "I don't think he took the marathon money."

She sighed. "And you won't believe how stupid I looked, finding that out."

"What happened?" Bert asked.

"Yeah," Flossie said. "You were so brave, going there alone."

Nan filled them in on her search of Mr. Potter's office—and how she got caught.

65

"It's a good thing he didn't have you arrested," Bert said.

"What if they stuck you in jail?" Freddie's eyes went big.

"Give me a break," Nan said. "I didn't steal anything. All I did was make a fool of myself."

"So now you really believe Mr. Potter didn't take the money?" Bert asked.

"I was so sure of it." Nan shrugged. "But he explained everything."

"Maybe he wasn't telling the truth," Flossie suggested.

"I think he was," Nan said. "He could have thrown me out of his office. But he let me stay, and he talked to me." She shook her head. "I'm so embarrassed. Mr. Potter had written a letter to the newspaper. He wanted everyone to know about the job I did. I saw it."

"I guess he won't be sending that now, huh?" Freddie's voice was sad.

"I don't know," Nan said. "And I still don't know who stole that money."

"Jackson Winters," Bert said promptly. He stood up and began pacing. "He's the only one left."

Nan looked up. "Did you go back to Mr. Winters's today?"

"Yeah." Bert didn't look happy. "But nobody was around."

"And you still think Mr. Winters stole the money while he was driving?" Nan asked.

"He's the only one left," Bert reminded her.

"That must have been some trick," Nan said. "He had to reach through the door, open the chest without tearing it up, steal the money, and put the newspaper inside. And he still had to drive the truck."

"Maybe he steers with his feet," Flossie suggested.

"Don't be silly," Freddie said.

"His knees?" Flossie asked.

"He could have had another box," Bert said. Then he stopped. "But where would he hide it? There's not much room in that cab." He sighed. His whole idea was crashing.

"I don't think the money was in the truck," Freddie said. "We ran past it on our way to the finish line."

"Yeah," Flossie said. "It was wide open. I could look inside and everything."

"So could I," Freddie mumbled, "and there was something—"

Bert flopped on the ground beside him, cutting him off. "This is just great! We started out with all these suspects. Now we don't have any."

"We must have missed something," Nan said.

"But what?" Bert asked.

They sat quietly for a few minutes, thinking.

Then Nan said, "Got it!"

"You know what we missed?" Flossie asked.

"No," Nan said. "But I know a way to find out what it is."

Bert stared at her. "How?"

Nan smiled. "We'll commit the crime again!"

9

The Scene of the Crime

"We're going to do *what?*" Flossie couldn't believe her ears.

"Reenact the crime," Nan said.

"Re and who?" Flossie said.

"*Reenact* it," Bert explained. "We'll do everything the same way it happened on the day of the marathon."

"And we'll see what we've missed!" Freddie said. "*I* knew what it meant."

"You did not," Flossie said.

"Did, too," Freddie said.

"Come on, guys," Nan cut in. "We need your help. The first thing we have to do is make a new treasure chest."

"There's an extra cardboard box in the

garage," Bert said. "We even have some crepe paper left over."

The twins hurried to the garage.

Nan taped the cardboard box shut on all sides. Then Freddie and Flossie covered it with blue crepe paper. Finally, when it was completely covered, Bert cut a slot in the top.

"Just like the old one," he said.

"Now," Nan said, "let's cut up some newspaper. That will be our money."

The twins cut up old newspaper in the shape of the blue charity envelopes. They stuffed the "envelopes" into the chest.

"Tomorrow is Saturday," Nan said. "We'll get up early, go to City Hall, and start from there. Each of us will be one of the committee members."

"Great idea," Flossie said. "I'll be Mrs. Cox and steal the money."

"No, you won't," Nan said. "We're going to watch to see where someone *could* have stolen the money."

"But what about the Lakeport High School Band?" Freddie asked.

"You have a plastic horn," Nan said. "You can be the band, too."

"Great!" Freddie grinned.

"We forgot something else," Bert said.

"What's that?" Nan asked.

"We don't have an armored truck."

Nan was silent for a moment. "That *is* a problem," she said. "I don't suppose we could borrow Mr. Winters's."

Bert shook his head.

"We could use our bikes," Freddie suggested.

"That's not the same thing," Bert said.

Flossie jumped up. "You could pull me in my wagon," she said.

"Flossie, you're a real genius," Bert said. "I'll tie your wagon to my bike and pull you. It'll be just like Mr. Winters's armored truck—with me in the cab and you in the back."

"*I'm* the one who thought of using our bikes," Freddie grumbled.

"So, we're set," Nan said. "By this time tomorrow, we'll know who stole the marathon money."

The twins were eating cold cereal when Mr. and Mrs. Bobbsey came into the kitchen the next morning.

"What's this?" said Mr. Bobbsey. "You're all up early—even Flossie."

Flossie yawned. "We're going to solve the mystery today."

"I figured as much," said Mrs. Bobbsey.

The twins grinned. They excused themselves and headed for the garage.

Nan tied the treasure chest to her bicycle.

Bert tied Flossie's wagon to his bike, and Flossie climbed in.

Freddie tooted a few notes on his horn.

"Ready, everybody?" Nan asked.

"Wait a minute," Flossie said. "This isn't comfortable." She got out of the wagon and began poking around the garage.

"What now?" Bert asked.

"Found it!" Flossie said. She held up an old rug. "I'm going to sit on this," she said. She laid the rug inside the wagon and sat down again.

"Fine," Bert said. "Just like the real truck." He got back on his bicycle. "Let's move." They set off for City Hall.

When they arrived, no one was around.

"Good," Nan said. "We'll be able to reenact the crime without anyone getting in the way."

"Where do we start?" Flossie asked.

"Freddie, you go to the top of the stairs. Pretend you're Mr. Potter in his office," Nan said. She handed him the treasure chest. "I'll go a few steps below you and pretend to be the mayor in his office."

"Right," Freddie said. He took the chest and climbed to the top of the stairs.

Nan followed him, but stopped five steps below. "Bert, you and Flossie pull up in front of City Hall and be waiting," she yelled.

Bert circled into position with the bicycle and wagon. "We're ready!"

"Ready!" Flossie repeated.

"Freddie!" Nan called. "It's the night before the marathon. You come to my office and hand over the treasure chest."

"Got it," Freddie said. He walked down the steps to Nan and handed her the treasure chest.

"Thank you, Mr. Potter," she said, trying to sound like Mayor Childress. "Now take your plastic horn and get in front of Bert," she told him in her own voice. "You're the band now."

Freddie bounded down the steps. Waving his horn, he took his position as the Lakeport High School Band.

"Okay," Nan said. "It's now the morning of the marathon. I, Mayor Childress, am now about to hand over the treasure chest to Jackson Winters. He'll take it in his armored truck to the winner's platform." She walked to the bottom of the steps and handed the chest to Bert.

"And I, Jackson Winters," Bert said, "will hand over the chest to my trusted employee, Hank Caldwell. He will lock it up with him in the back of my armored truck." Bert handed the treasure chest to Flossie.

"And I, Hank Caldwell, will guard this chest with my life," Flossie said.

Bert got on his bicycle. "Get ready, Lakeport

High School Band," he called to Freddie. "Start playing and lead us to the winner's platform."

"Hold it!" Nan yelled. "I need to get there first, so I can be Mrs. Cox." She rushed to her bike and pedaled away.

Toot! Toot! Toot! Freddie blared his horn as loudly as he could.

Bert started pedaling.

Flossie held onto the treasure chest.

Toot! Toot! Toot!

"Can't you walk any faster, Freddie?" Bert yelled. "I can't keep my balance if I have to go this slowly."

"I'm supposed to be marching," Freddie answered, "not running."

"Well, march a little faster, please," Bert said.

"Yuck," Flossie said. "I'm getting blue stuff all over my hands."

Bert turned his head. "It's just from the crepe paper," he said. "It'll wash off."

Toot! Toot! "Hey!" Freddie yelled. "You nearly ran me over."

Bert stopped just in time. "Sorry." He kept his eyes on the road. Soon they reached the spot where the winner's platform had been.

"They took down the platform," Nan said. "So we'll have to pretend that, too." She stepped forward. "Okay, the band and the armored truck have arrived. Now Mr. Winters

hands over the treasure chest to Mrs. Cox."

"No, no," Flossie spoke up. "Hank Caldwell hands it to her. He's locked inside the armored truck."

Bert nodded. "And he's the only one who can open the door."

"Okay," Flossie said. She began pulling up the rug she'd been sitting on.

"What are you doing?" Freddie asked.

"I hid the key under the carpet," Flossie said. "I'm just getting it out."

Bert stared at her for a long minute.

Flossie pretended to unlock the door from inside. She stepped out of the wagon and walked up to the make-believe winner's platform. Then she handed Nan the treasure chest.

"Now I, Mrs. Cox," Nan said, "will place the chest on this table until the end of the marathon. Then the mayor will open it."

Bert, Freddie, Flossie, and Nan stood for a moment. "Okay," Nan said, "it's the end of the marathon. The winners are all here beside me.

"I, Mayor Childress, shall now open the treasure chest." Nan tore open the cardboard box. "It's full of cut-up newspaper!" she shouted. "The money's gone!"

Nobody said anything for a minute.

"Okay," Freddie finally said. "We did everything just like the first time. Do we know who stole the money?"

"I think we do," Bert said slowly. "And Flossie is the one who showed us."

"Me?" Flossie said. "What did I do?"

Nan turned to her brother. Then she began to grin. "We'll explain it all," she said. "While we tell Lieutenant Pike!"

10

Gotcha!

The police car pulled up in front of Winters Armored Truck Service. Lieutenant Pike shook his head. "I must be crazy," he said to Bert. "How did I let you kids talk me into coming here? We can't just go in and accuse someone of stealing that money. We need evidence."

"We *have* to go inside," Nan said. "That's where the evidence is."

"Yeah," Freddie said. "I even saw it on the day of the marathon. But I didn't realize what it was."

"You have to admit, our idea fits all the facts," Bert said.

Lieutenant Pike sighed. "We checked out all the committee members. I thought we almost had our man when I learned about Harrison

Potter's aunt. But his story about selling stock panned out."

The lieutenant pulled open the patrol car door. "Okay, we'll go in. But you kids stay behind me. Things could get serious." He got out of the car and headed for the office.

The twins were right behind him.

Hank Caldwell looked up. He had a surprised expression on his face. "Is anything wrong?" he asked the lieutenant.

Lieutenant Pike looked at the twins, then back at Hank. "I'd like to examine the armored truck," he said.

"Uh, why?" Hank asked.

"What's going on here?" Jackson Winters stepped into the front office.

"I'm sorry to disturb you, Mr. Winters," Lieutenant Pike said. "But the Bobbseys suggested"—he swallowed and went on—"that your truck might have something to do with the theft of the marathon money."

"My truck?" said Mr. Winters. He glared at the twins. "Are you accusing me of stealing that money?"

Nan stepped forward. "No, sir," she said. "But we think your truck was involved. All we want to do is examine it."

"I don't like this at all," said Mr. Winters. "Does Chief Smith know you're here?"

"This sounds like some kind of trick to me,"

said Hank. "I don't think you should let them look at the truck. You have your rights. Let them get a search warrant."

Mr. Winters shook his head. "We don't have anything to hide." He looked at the twins and shrugged. "Come on, let's take a look," he said. "The truck is parked in the garage."

Lieutenant Pike and the twins followed Mr. Winters. Hank trailed along behind.

"If you're wrong . . ." whispered the lieutenant.

Flossie took his hand. "Have we ever been wrong before?"

"There's always a first time," Lieutenant Pike said darkly.

"There it is," said Mr. Winters. "What did you want to see?"

"We'd like a look inside the back," Bert said. "Could you give us the key?"

"Don't have it," said Mr. Winters. "Hank's the one who rides in back." He turned around. "Hank, open the door."

"I—I'm not sure where the key is," said Hank.

"Well, you'd better find it," said Mr. Winters. "And quick."

"Is there another key?" Nan asked.

"There's one in the safe," said Mr. Winters, "but—"

"Uh, here it is," said Hank. He took the key out of his pocket and handed it over.

Mr. Winters unlocked the back door of the armored truck. "There it is," he said.

"Hey," Nan said, peeking in. "It looks very cozy in there, with that rug."

"Does this carpet come up?" Bert asked.

"Sure," said Mr. Winters. He lifted up one side of the carpet.

"Look!" Bert's hand went to the edge of the rug. "There's a piece of paper caught here." He pulled the tiny scrap loose, then held it up. "It's blue crepe paper."

"So what?" said Hank.

"Would you kids please explain what's going on?" said Lieutenant Pike.

"I'd like to know, too," said Mr. Winters.

"We reenacted the crime today," Flossie said.

"That's right," Freddie added. "We all played different roles. I was the Lakeport High School Band and Mr. Potter."

Mr. Winters stared at the twins. "Is this a joke?"

"It helped us solve the mystery," Nan said.

Hank Caldwell stepped closer. "Oh, yeah? A bunch of dumb kids?"

"Keep quiet, Hank," ordered Mr. Winters. "Go on, Nan."

"Flossie had the treasure chest in her wagon,"

Nan explained. "That was the armored truck. We didn't think anything about it until we reached the winner's platform. That's when we told her to pretend to unlock the door and get out."

"So?" said Hank.

Mr. Winters gave him a stern look.

"That's when Flossie lifted up the rug she'd been sitting on," Bert said.

"The wagon was hard," Flossie explained. "I put a rug down to sit on."

"But why did you lift up the rug?" asked the lieutenant.

"That was my hiding place for the key," Flossie said.

"But it made me think about the carpet in the armored truck," Bert said. "And how *it* could be used as a hiding place."

"You're guessing." Hank's face was turning pale.

"But I think we're guessing right," Bert said.

"Keep going," said Lieutenant Pike.

"There was only one time when the chest was out of sight on marathon day," Bert said. "That was when it was locked up with Hank."

Hank was shouting now. "If I stole that money, then how'd I get it out of the box without tearing it up?"

"You tell him, Nan," Freddie said.

"You *did* tear up the box," Nan said.

Hank looked at Mr. Winters. "You saw the box I gave to Mrs. Cox. It wasn't torn at all!"

"*That* one wasn't torn," Nan agreed. "Because it was a *duplicate*. You did what we did last night—made another chest, and filled it with cut-up newspaper."

"You're the one who keeps the key to the back of the truck," Bert said. "So it was no problem to hide the chest you made in there. Then you substituted it for Nan's."

"Oh, yeah?" Hank was desperate now. "And where did it go?"

"That's easy," Nan said. "You flattened out the real chest and hid it under the carpet."

"Along with the money," Bert added. "Then, even if anyone got suspicious and looked inside, they'd see nothing. All you had to do was wait until no one was around. Then you could get at the money."

"And that's why we found that little piece of paper, stuck to the rug," Nan said. "It's from the original treasure chest, which you hid under the carpet."

"Flossie and I saw the armored car parked over by some bushes during the marathon," Freddie said. "The back door was open. And there was blue paper by the rear wheel!"

"And how about the time *I* looked into the truck?" Bert asked. "You picked up something—*a piece of blue paper.*"

"Sure, try and blame me." Hank was breathing heavily. "But what about *her?*" He pointed at Nan. "I saw her with the marathon money—*three envelopes.* And that was *after* the robbery."

"Hank," Nan said quietly, "I only had *one* envelope in my hand when I answered the door. How do you know how many envelopes came to my house?"

"I—I—" Hank turned to run. But Lieutenant Pike had already grabbed his arm.

Hank sagged. "Well, I almost got away with it."

"You were half-smart," said Lieutenant Pike. "But that's not smart enough!" He took out his handcuffs and snapped them on Hank's wrists. Then he read Hank his rights.

"Why did you steal the money?" asked Mr. Winters.

Hank shrugged. "It seemed like an easy way to get my hands on some big bucks. More than four thousand dollars."

"Where's the money now?" Nan asked.

"At my house," Hank said, "under the rug."

"Boy, when he gets a good idea, he sticks with it," Bert whispered.

"Four thousand dollars, eh?" Mr. Winters took out his checkbook and started writing. When he finished, he handed the check to Nan.

Her eyes popped when she read the amount. "This—this is for—"

"*Another* four thousand dollars," said Mr. Winters. "Thanks to me, the needy children of Lakeport almost lost that amount. Now they'll be sure to get it."

"Thank you!" Nan said.

"See!" Flossie said. "I told you Mr. Winters wasn't a miser."

The other twins looked at each other in horror.

But Mr. Winters was laughing out loud. "Well, now you know," he said.

"That's right," Nan said. "And thanks to you, the Lakeport Kids' Mini-Marathon is a runaway success!"